Contents

SUSAN GATES

DINOSAUR GARDEN

Illustrated by
Georgie Birkett

OXFORD
UNIVERSITY PRESS

OXFORD

UNIVERSITY PRESS

Great Clarendon Street, Oxford OX2 6DP

Oxford University Press is a department of the University of Oxford.
It furthers the University's objective of excellence in research, scholarship,
and education by publishing worldwide in

Oxford New York

Athens Auckland Bangkok Bogotá Buenos Aires Calcutta
Cape Town Chennai Dar es Salaam Delhi Florence Hong Kong Istanbul
Karachi Kuala Lumpur Madrid Melbourne Mexico City Mumbai
Nairobi Paris São Paulo Shanghai Singapore Taipei Tokyo Toronto Warsaw

and associated companies in Berlin Ibadan

Oxford is a trade mark of Oxford University Press
in the UK and in certain other countries

British Library Cataloguing in Publication Data
Data available

ISBN 0 19 915950 5

Printed in Hong Kong

Available in packs

Year 4 / Primary 5 Pack of Six (one of each book)   ISBN 0 19 915955 6
Year 4 / Primary 5 Class Pack (six of each book)   ISBN 0 19 915956 4

1

Footprints on Stone

I opened my eyes. It was still dark. Why had I woken up so early? In a sudden flash, my bedroom lit up with blue light, then went dark again. There was a terrific storm outside.

I could hear waves crashing on the seashore. I thought, "There'll be lots of interesting things washed up on the beach tomorrow."

Next day, I didn't even stop to have breakfast. "Here, Nipper!" I yelled. Nipper's our dog. We got him from a dogs' home. Nobody else wanted him but we think he's the best dog in the world.

"Where are you going?" asked Annie, my little sister.

I groaned. "Down to the beach."

I knew she was going to tag along. If I tried to say "No," she'd run to Mum and say, "Liam's being horrid to me!"

"Come on then," I said sighing.

Nipper raced up and down chasing seagulls. I went beachcombing.

"What are these?" said Annie. She was pointing to some strange markings on a big, flat rock.

I turned to look.

"They're footprints!" I said. "They must have been uncovered by the storm."

They were all over the rock. Some big, some little. Nipper came up and barked at them.

"It's all right, boy," I said. I was really excited. I thought, "They can't be what I think they are!"

"I think they're fossil dinosaur footprints," I told Annie.

Her hands flew to her mouth. Her eyes went wide. "Do you mean *T Rex*?" she asked me. *T Rex* is the only dinosaur she knows.

"There are loads of different kinds of dinosaurs," I told her. "I can't tell which they are. Only dinosaur experts can tell."

Nipper was still barking. I thought, "What's wrong with him?" Something must have scared him. I looked round. But our beach is a lonely place. There was nobody here but us.

"Be quiet, Nipper," I said.

I knelt down by the footprints. What a brilliant discovery! The more I looked at them, the more I knew I was right.

They were dinosaur footprints. I'd found fossils before on this beach but nothing as amazing as this!

Nipper sniffed at them. He started growling like mad.

I dragged him away by his collar. "They won't hurt you, Nipper. They're millions of years old."

But he raced off home with his tail between his legs. Annie started to go too. "I'm going to tell Mum and Dad!"

I said, "No, not yet. Let's keep it a secret."

Annie likes secrets. So she didn't kick up a fuss. She just said, "All right. I won't tell anyone. Cross my heart and hope to die."

2

The Seeds

That afternoon Mum said, "Don't forget you're going out with Grandad and Gran."

"Oh no," I moaned. "Do I have to? Why can't Annie go with them?"

I was frantic to get down to the beach again to see my dinosaur footprints. I'd been thinking about them all through lunch.

Mum said, "Annie's going to a birthday party."

I said, "Aww, Mum."

But I knew by the look on her face that there was no point in arguing.

I asked Gran and Grandad, "Can we go down to the beach?"

Grandad said, "Gran wants to go to a garden centre. To get some plant pots."

I mumbled, "Oh no, not a boring garden centre."

"What's that?" said Gran sharply. "We might call at the beach on the way back. If we've got time."

I sat in the back of the car in a bad mood. But I daren't be too sulky. I knew Gran would report back to Mum.

"Stop here!" said Gran suddenly.

Grandad screeched to a halt. "We're not at the garden centre yet!"

"I know," said Gran. "But I've just

seen another one. It says CLOSING DOWN SALE. LAST DAY. Come on, we might get some bargains."

"Where did that place spring from?" said Grandad. "I've never seen it before."

I trailed after them into the garden centre. They went into one greenhouse. I wandered into another.

I thought straightaway, "I don't like this place."

There were no other visitors. No one around at all. A fly went *buzzz*! against the glass. It made me jump. Everything was covered in dust – all the plant pots and bags of compost – as if no one had been here for years and years.

I bumped into a rack of seed packets. They fell all over the floor. I bent down to pick them up. GROW YOUR OWN BUTTERFLY GARDEN, said the packet I was holding. *Attract butterflies to your garden, by growing plants they love to feed on.*

"Boring," I thought as I put it back on the rack. I bent to pick up another packet. GROW YOUR OWN DINOSAUR GARDEN, it said.

"Huh?" I read it again. It still said the same thing. I thought my eyes were playing tricks.

GROW
YOUR OWN
BUTTERFLY
GARDEN

GROW
YOUR OWN
DINOSAUR
GARDEN

I turned the packet over. *Attract dinosaurs to your garden*, it said, *by growing plants they love to feed on.*

I laughed out loud. "This is some kind of joke!"

It wasn't a very good joke either. No one would be fooled. Everyone knows that dinosaurs are extinct. I was going to put it back on the rack.

Then something made me change my mind. I thought, "Might as well buy it."

I went to the pay desk. There was nobody there. There was no price on the packet of seeds. I had 50p in my pocket. I left it on the pay desk and rushed out of the greenhouse.

"Mind what you're doing!" It was Gran. I was really pleased to see her. "Are we going now?" I asked. I had to get out of that creepy place.

I didn't tell Gran about the *Grow
Your Own Dinosaur Garden* seeds.
She'd only say, "Liam, I thought you
had more sense. What a terrible waste of
your pocket money!" She'd be right, too.

Gran kept her promise. We stopped
at the beach on our way home.

"Aren't you going to get out and
play?" she asked me.

But I couldn't believe my eyes. I was
horrified!

My dinosaur footprints had been discovered – by somebody else, and whoever it was hadn't kept it a secret. The beach was already swarming with people and the worst thing was, they'd put ropes around the footprints and KEEP OFF signs so I couldn't get to them! And I was the one who'd found them first.

"I don't want to play," I told Gran. "Just take me home."

Gran shook her head, as if to say, "Kids these days. There's no pleasing them, is there?"

3
Success Guaranteed

I felt really bad about those dinosaur footprints. As if something precious had been taken away from me and given to other people.

I was up in my bedroom, giving Nipper a good hug, when Annie crept in.

"You don't need to keep our secret any more," I said, bitterly. "The whole world knows about the dinosaur footprints. It'll probably be on telly tonight!"

"I'm really sorry, Liam," said Annie. She's only little, but she understood how I felt. Then she said, "What's this?" She picked up the packet of seeds from my bed.

"Oh, those!" I said. "I bought them in a garden centre this afternoon. I must have been mad. What a waste of money."

But she seemed really interested. "*Attract dinosaurs to your garden*," she read. Then she said, "What's this word say?"

"It says *guaranteed*," I told her impatiently. "*Success guaranteed*."

I just wanted her to go away. So I could carry on feeling sorry for myself about the dinosaur footprints.

"Well, why don't we plant them

then?" she said. "Look it says, *super fast growing seeds*. We won't have to wait for long."

"Ha, ha!" I laughed. "You must be joking!"

She really believed what it said on the packet! As if words couldn't lie!

"Go on, Liam," she said. "You're really sad about those dinosaur footprints. This will make up for it. This'll be even better. You can have your very own dinosaurs!"

I sighed. "I told you, it's some kind of joke."

But Annie had that stubborn look in her eyes. The one she gets when you don't do what she wants. "I'll tell Mum you're being horrid," she said.

I gave another sigh. There was no way out of it. "Come on, Nipper," I said. "We've got some planting to do."

Our garden is really big and overgrown. Mum and Dad hardly ever go out there. They're not interested in gardening. I tore open the packet and tipped some seeds into my hand.

It had a list of what they were on the packet: *Gingkoes, tree-ferns, monkey puzzles.*

"Is that what dinosaurs eat?" demanded Annie.

"Yes," I had to admit. "It's what some of them eat."

"There you are then," she said. "I told you they would work. *Success guaranteed!*"

"Annie! It *can't* work! Dinosaurs are extinct!"

But she just wouldn't listen. Once she gets an idea in her head, nothing can shake it loose.

We planted the seeds. We made
holes with our
fingers and poked
them in.

Nipper didn't help much. He kept
trying to dig them up again.

"Go away, Nipper," I told him.

I thought, "What's wrong with that
dog? He's been acting funny all day."

After we planted the seeds, it rained

for days and days. We couldn't go out in the garden. I couldn't go down to the beach. I didn't want to anyway. Not now the dinosaur footprints weren't a secret anymore.

One day I found Annie with her elbows on the window sill, staring out into the garden. "What are you looking for?" I asked her.

"I'm looking to see if those dinosaur plants have grown."

I laughed. "What are you doing that for? You don't believe all that stuff it said on the packet, do you?"

But Annie didn't answer.

Next day, the rain cleared. The sky was blue. You could see the sea just beyond the woods, sparkling in the sunshine. Nipper raced round my legs, barking. He wanted a walk on the beach.

"We'll go as far as the woods," I told him. I couldn't face going down to the beach.

Then Annie came running into my bedroom. She was jiggling about with excitement. "The dinosaur plants have grown!" she said.

"You're kidding me."

"Come and look!"

It was true. Those seeds had grown super fast, just as it promised they would on the packet. I don't know anything about plants, but even I could see that they were weird, primitive-looking things. They were all bright green. Some were ferny, some spiny, some had fat, jungly leaves.

I was really surprised. I didn't think anything would grow at all.

"It's brilliant!" said Annie dancing about. "Isn't it, Liam?"

I pretended to search round the garden. "I don't see any dinosaurs yet!" I told her.

"Don't make fun of me, Liam," begged Annie.

I stopped laughing at her. I tried to talk to her seriously. "Annie, listen to me. Just because the seeds have grown, it doesn't mean that dinosaurs will come. How can they? They don't exist any more."

She scowled at me.

"It's not my fault," I said. "I've tried to tell you. Just don't be disappointed when they don't turn up, that's all!"

4

Dinosaur Music

Very late that night, someone came bursting into my bedroom. They woke me up.

Someone shouted in my ear, "Get up, Liam!"

"Go away," I said, sleepily.

I forced my eyes open. It was Annie. She was shaking my arm.

"They're here," she said. "The dinosaurs are here!"

"Go back to bed, Annie. You've been dreaming."

"I haven't... They're really here."

What could I do? I let her drag me over to the window. She pulled back the curtains. The garden looked silvery blue in the moonlight.

I couldn't believe it. There was a small herd of dinosaurs on our lawn.

"This isn't real!" I told myself.

"Come on," said Annie, wild with excitement. "Let's go outside."

I followed Annie downstairs. I was in a daze, moving like a robot. Annie unlocked the back door.

I thought, "We shouldn't be doing this," but there were no sounds from upstairs. Mum and Dad were asleep.

"See," said Annie, as if she hadn't doubted it for a second. "I told you dinosaurs would come."

We stood watching from the doorway. I couldn't deny it any longer. There really were dinosaurs in my back garden. They were grazing on the tender young tree-ferns and gingko plants. Pulling them up and munching them like cows.

"Let's go closer," whispered Annie.

"Wait!" I said, grabbing her arm.

My mind seemed suddenly to have unfrozen. I was frantically thinking, "Is it safe to go out there?" They looked like fierce, giant lizards, but they weren't very big, not *T rex* size and they seemed peaceful, munching away on the plants. I decided, "They won't hurt us."

So we walked out among the dinosaurs. I had butterflies in my stomach. I was so nervous, so thrilled, I could hardly breathe. I whispered to

Annie, "I know what these are!" I remembered them from my school library book. They all had strange bony crests on their heads.

"They're *Pachycephalosaurus*!" I said in an awed voice.

"Packyseffa- what?" asked Annie.

Suddenly one of them stood upright.

It tipped its lizard head back. It made a gentle booming sound, like blowing across the top of a giant bottle.

"Just like a didgeridoo!" I whispered.

Another answered. Then another. "They're calling to each other," I told Annie.

Annie said, "It's like magic!" She had a big, beaming smile on her face. She walked out onto the lawn. "Annie," I said. "Come back!" She was moving too far away from the house. What if we had to run back?

But there didn't seem to be any danger. The dinosaurs didn't harm her. They carried on grazing and calling, like the foghorns of ships far out at sea.

Annie started dancing, holding out her arms and dancing in the

moonlight to
dinosaur music.
I stood near
the doorway
watching.
I forgot
where I
was. I
forgot
I was
in the
twenty-
first
century.
Then,
suddenly
the spell
was broken.

"Liam!" That was Dad's voice. That meant trouble!

"Are you out of bed?" he yelled from upstairs.

"Annie," I hissed as loud as I dared. "Come back! Where's Nipper?"

Nipper was cowering by my feet. He hadn't gone far out into the garden. I stooped down to stroke him. "They won't hurt you, boy," I told him.

"Woof! Woof!" barked Nipper.

The gentle *Pachycephalosaurus* were startled. They fled out of our garden into the wood. Just in time. I could hear Dad moving about upstairs.

Annie and I crept quietly back into the house, before Dad found out we'd been gone.

5

Velociraptor!

They came back the next night, at midnight. This time, Annie and I were waiting. We were watching from the kitchen window. Mum and Dad were in bed asleep.

Why didn't we tell Mum and Dad about the *Pachycephalosaurus*? For the same reason we didn't tell about the dinosaur footprints. We didn't want to share our dinosaurs with grown ups.

Not even with Mum and Dad.

"They're here," whispered Annie.

I was trembling with excitement. I'd been really scared – scared they wouldn't come at all.

One by one, the shy, plant-eating dinosaurs came out of the wood. They craned their long necks around. They were looking for danger.

"It's all right," Annie said, as if they could hear her. "You're safe in our garden. Nothing can hurt you."

We opened the back door very quietly. "I'm going to stroke one tonight," said Annie. "I'm going to make friends with them."

Nipper was with us. He was shivering, making soft, whining noises.

I said, "Nipper, it's all right. They eat tree-ferns, not dogs!" I wanted him to make friends with the dinosaurs too.

But something was wrong. The
Pachycephalosaurus were restless. They
were booming to each other, but these
weren't friendly calls like last night.
They sounded like alarm signals.

"What's the matter with them?"
asked Annie.

There was a quivering in the trees
at the edge of the wood. What was it?

Some of the *Pachycephalosaurus*
started to run.

"Come back," Annie begged them.
"Don't you like our garden?"

I couldn't see what had startled
them.

By my side, Nipper was growling.
"What's up boy?" I asked him.

Branches crashed. Something sprang

into the garden. It was smaller than
Pachycephalosaurus. It had a thin,
snaky head and slashing claws.
It moved with deadly speed.

"*Velociraptor*!" I
whispered.

It had come hunting.

"Stay here!" I said, dragging Annie back.

"It's going to eat my dinosaurs!" she cried, tugging herself free. She had seen those savage teeth.

"No, stay here!" I told her again. "Or it'll eat you!"

Too late. The *Velociraptor* was sniffing the air. It had picked up our scent. The last of the plant-eating dinosaurs vanished into the wood. The raptor bounded across our lawn.

"Don't move," I hissed at Annie.

I wanted to panic. I wanted to run screaming for the house. But they only pounce if you move. My dinosaur book said that. I thought, "I hope that book's right."

The raptor was really close. We could smell its rotten breath, see its beady, shark-like eyes. It was looking

straight into my face. My whole body
started shaking. I couldn't stop it.

It snarled. It was going to
attack!

"Grrrr!" Nipper rushed out from
behind me, growling.

The raptor's head swivelled round. It had found its dinner.

"Nipper!" shouted Annie. There was nothing we could do.

Nipper shot off across the garden, but that raptor sprinted after him, fast as a cheetah.

"It's going to get him!" I couldn't bear to watch.

Nipper wriggled through a gap in the hedge. The raptor cleared it in one great, springy leap.

The wood swallowed them up. We heard crashing sounds. Then there was silence.

Annie started to cry.

"I bet Nipper's escaped," I told her. I wanted to comfort her, but I knew my voice sounded hopeless.

That night I was tossing and turning in bed, thinking about Nipper.

I didn't get any sleep at all.

Just before dawn there was another terrific storm. Wind biffed our house like a punch bag. I could hear waves thunder on the beach.

Through the wind and the rain I thought I heard something. I listened hard. I heard dinosaurs! No doubt about it. Raptors snarling and growling. *Pachycephalosaurus* booming like foghorns. The sounds they made in the storm grew fainter and fainter. Then died away altogether.

6

Nipper

At breakfast I staggered downstairs.
"You look worn out," said Mum. "Did
the storm keep you awake?"

"Yes," I lied.

Then I said, "Is Nipper around?"

"Come to think of it," said Mum,
"I haven't seen him at all this
morning."

Mum started saying something else
to me. I was only half-listening.

"What a shame," she said. "That

storm last night covered the dinosaur footprints. You know, the ones down on the beach. They're buried under tons of sand again, and the experts had only just found out what dinosaurs made them."

I was paying attention now. Little lights had come on in my brain.

"There was a raptor, wasn't there?" I asked. "And some *Pachycephalosaurus*?"

"How did you know that?" said Mum. "Was it on telly?"

I found Annie in the garden.

"What are you doing?" I asked her.

She was pulling up all the dinosaur plants and throwing them onto a big heap in the middle of the lawn.

"I'm destroying them!" she said. "I don't want those dinosaurs to come back! If they hadn't come Nipper would still be alive!"

"I don't think they're going to come back anyway," I said.

"What do you mean?" sniffed Annie. She wiped her nose on her sleeve. "I can't stop crying," she said. "Every time I think about Nipper I cry."

I tried to explain.

"I think the dinosaurs came to our garden because of the plants – but they came back through *time* because of the footprints. I don't know how, but when those footprints were uncovered it was like a door opening. The dinosaurs walked through it from prehistory. Now the footprints have gone again, they're gone too. They've been whisked back to Jurassic times. I heard it happening last night, in the storm."

I don't think Annie was really

listening. "Nipper saved our lives," she said.

"I know," I told her. "He was a hero."

Like Annie, I couldn't get Nipper out of my mind. I thought, "I'll walk down to the beach." There was nothing to see now the footprints were gone, but at least it was something to do.

I walked through the wood. I wasn't afraid of that raptor. The wood didn't feel dangerous. The raptor had gone, back to prehistoric times.

There was a scuffling in the leaves.

"Nipper!" I yelled.

He came crawling out of a rabbit hole. His coat was full of twigs and sticky jacks. He looked really sorry for himself.

"You're alive!"

He wagged his tail feebly.

I was so happy I couldn't stop hugging him. I picked him up and went racing back to our garden.

"Annie!" I was shouting as I ran. "Annie! Guess who I've brought to see you!"

7

What would you do?

It had been two weeks since the
Pachycephalosaurus came into our
garden, and the raptor came to hunt
them and nearly got us and Nipper
instead. Annie and I were out in the
car with Gran and Grandad. We were
going up a twisty road.

"Wait a minute," said Gran.
"Wasn't that garden centre here? The
one that had a closing down sale?"

"It *was* here," said Grandad. "But where is it now?"

There was no sign at all of that garden centre. It was as if it had never existed. It seemed to have vanished off the face of the earth.

"Good!" Annie whispered to me in the back of the car. "That means no one can buy any more of those special seeds. No one can grow their own dinosaur garden."

I thought, "That's where you're wrong."

I hadn't told Annie, but when we planted our dinosaur garden we didn't use all the seeds. I still had half a packet left.

One day there will be another storm, and those footprints might be uncovered. Shall I plant some seeds? So I can see dinosaurs again?

A sensible voice in my head says, "No, Liam. How can you think such a thing? What about that raptor? It would be terribly dangerous!"

But it would be really exciting wouldn't it? It would be every kid's dream.

I don't know what I'll do when the time comes. What would you do? If you had a chance to see living, breathing dinosaurs in your back garden?

About the author

I know that the boy in this book says that garden centres are boring. My children think so too. But I have to admit that I got the idea for this story in a garden centre. I saw tree-ferns for sale – the kind of plants that some dinosaurs liked to eat. Then I picked up a packet of seeds that said, "Attract Butterflies to your Garden". And so *Dinosaur Garden* was born.

I love that magical moment when two little ideas join together to make one big beast of an idea!